For Chiqui
D.S.
For my family
J.R.

Aladdin Books
Macmillan Publishing Company
866 Third Avenue, New York, NY 10022
First published 1988 in Great Britain by Walker Books Ltd., London
First American edition 1988
First Aladdin Books edition 1989

A B C D   0 1 2 3

Library of Congress Cataloging-in-Publication Data

Sheldon, Dyan.
I forgot.
Summary: Though he always seems to forget something that he's supposed to do,
Jake surprises his mother by remembering something really important.
[1. Memory—Fiction] I. Rogan, John, ill. II. Title.
PZ7.S54144Iaf 1989   [E]   88-19440
ISBN 0–689–71211–1 (pbk.)

I FORGOT

WRITTEN BY
DYAN SHELDON

ILLUSTRATED BY
JOHN ROGAN

Aladdin Books
MACMILLAN PUBLISHING COMPANY   NEW YORK

Jake was in a hurry this morning.

He put on his clothes.

He brushed his teeth.

But he forgot one thing....

"Oh, Jake," called his mother
as he rushed from the house.
"What about your shoes?"

Jake jumped on his bike
and raced to the stores.

He counted his change.

He even remembered to check his
packages before he left each store.
He forgot just one thing....

"Oh, Jake," sighed his mother when he ran into the house. "Don't tell me you came back without your bike."

Jake had something to wrap in a hurry.

He got out the paper and the scissors.

He got out the tape and
the basket of ribbons.

The one thing he forgot about
was the cat....

"Oh, Jake!" yelled his mother.
"Now look what you've done."

Jake had something to do in the garden.

He remembered to put on his boots.

He remembered to put on
his mother's gardening gloves.

But there was one thing
he didn't remember....

His mother appeared at the kitchen window. "Oh, Jake!" she shouted. "Just look at you. Don't come back in here with all that mud."

It was time to give the dog a bath.

Jake remembered not to put
too much water in the tub.

And he added the bubbles.

There was just one thing
he didn't remember....

"Oh, no!" wailed Jake's mother.
"I thought I told you
never to wash the dog in the house."

Jake called his mother into
the living room.

"Surprise! Surprise!" he shouted when she opened the door. "Happy birthday! Happy birthday! Happy birthday!"

"Oh, Jake!" His mother laughed.
"And I thought you forgot."